THE LOVE SUICIDES AT TAKAYAMA

by

Sheppard Ranbom

Finishing Line Press
Georgetown, Kentucky

THE LOVE SUICIDES
AT TAKAYAMA

Publisher: Leah Huete de Maines
Editor: Christen Kincaid
Cover Design: Michael Molanphy
Author Photo: Johanna Hjort

Order online: www.finishinglinepress.com
also available on amazon.com

Author inquiries and mail orders:
Finishing Line Press
PO Box 1626
Georgetown, Kentucky 40324
USA

Characters

- **NARRATOR**

- **KIMIKO MIYAGAWA**, age 25 and 36, artist

- **DANIEL SINGER**, age 19 and 30, an American writer of historical plays. His nickname in Japan is Tokubei (the name of a character in Chikamatsu's plays who is defeated by love and commits suicide). He might be considered a luftmensch, a dreamer with his head in the clouds who gets into trouble and needs others to help him

- **YASUKI NOMURA**, 55, film director and friend of Daniel

- **VELVA OGATA**, 30, actress and assistant film producer for Mr. Nomura

- **KARESHI**, 彼氏, 40, private detective hired by Mr. Miyagawa. (The name "Kareshi" means "boyfriend" in Japanese)

- **NOBORU MIYAGAWA**, 66, Kimiko's father, a retired squadron leader in the Imperial Air Force in World War II and current head of the agricultural research station in Takayama

- **REIKO MIYAGAWA**, 64, Kimiko's mother

- **MRS. ITO**, 64, runs a confectionary kiosk at the site of a major in shrine Takayama. Her part is played by the same person who plays Mrs. Miyagawa

- **NEWSMAN**, played by the same person who is the narrator

- **TWO SWORDSMEN**

The play introduces Chikamatsu, a bunraku puppet.

The Love Suicides at Takayama is dedicated to the memories of two great friends, Yasuki Hamano and George C. Hudson.

Hamano, a professor at Tokyo University of Technology, was an authority on cinema, anime films, media, and education. He was a production assistant on two of Kurosawa's later films and served as a director of the Akira Kurosawa Foundation. Many years ago, he suggested that I turn the backstory of this play into a film. I have sought to honor his wish and hope that I have captured the comedy and sadness he envisioned.

George Hudson was my professor at Colgate University, who, out of the blue, invited me to participate in his Japanese study group in Kyoto where I was immersed in learning the Japanese language as well as Japanese aesthetics and poetry. He took us to our first performances of the Noh, Kabuki and bunraku theatres. A Renaissance man whose erudition and broad interests influenced generations of students, George was also my guide to 19th century British literature, Southern literature, and the art museums of Moscow and St. Petersburg.

> In the evening darkness
> he comes from the distance
> bringing a lamp.
> —*adapted from Bashō*

Foreword

The impetus for this play was an experience I had many years ago in Japan. I had taken a train from Tokyo to Nagoya and planned to switch lines to the old city of Takayama in the Japanese Alps. When I reached Nagoya, I disembarked into the underground shopping area and called my girlfriend to see if I could visit her family before returning to America. She told me that I should not so much as set foot in the next prefecture, because she was afraid of what her father might do.

The Love Suicides at Takayama is a comedy that imagines what might have happened if I had continued my journey. It also pays homage to the love suicide tradition of Japan's most admired playwright, Chikamatsu Monzaemon (1653-1725), who wrote plays for the Kabuki and puppet theatre (*bunraku*).

I first became aware of Chikamatsu on reading *The Love Suicides at Sonezaki*, the three-act template from which Chikamatsu built his most successful domestic plays, and many of his major works in translation. According to Donald Keene, the grand interpreter of Japanese literature, the final scene of *The Love Suicides at Sonezaki*—the last walk of the lovers before their suicide—is one of the finest examples of Japanese poetry.

Chikamatsu believed that "art lies in the thin margin between reality and unreality." Art is not life, with its banality and randomness, but an illusion that can reflect emotional truths more closely than the real world.

Chikamatsu wrote more than 100 plays, and his domestic tragedies are notable because they are among the first mature dramas in world literature to focus on the common man—in Chikamatsu's case, an odd mixture of clerks and tradesmen, robbers and acolytes. Most of the domestic tragedies are set in the pleasure quarters and involve an indulgent young man and a courtesan who fall in love and want to see each other exclusively. Unable to purchase the woman's freedom or to give up their relationship, they take their lives.

The heart of the love suicide play is the final act, sometimes an extended poem, in which the playwright lifts his desperate puppets above their tawdry and constrained circumstances and gives them a dignified sendoff that speaks not only to their own tragedy but to the transient nature of our own lives. The playwright must create an illuminating clarity that allows the audience to join the lovers' final embrace and hold in abeyance the obstacles of social class, poverty, human failures, and the stigma of death by one's own hand. The ritual suicide is presented not simply as exiting this life but, in true Buddhist fashion, a rebirth.

I will leave for a dramaturg to identify the complete list of devices I borrowed from Chikamatsu that are buried in the bondo—the putty of composition and design—that holds this work together. The most important is the poetic *michiyuki*, the final walk of the lovers before they take their lives, which provides the structure of the last act. Other key elements of Chikamatsu's *Shinjū* (double suicide) plays include: the narrator who comments on the feelings of his characters; use of street sounds of the *demimonde*; the establishment of a rival who is interested in the female protagonist; misunderstandings across generations; and the use of go-betweens who connect the separated lovers.

While tales of misaligned fortunes caused by societal circumstance were Chikamatsu's stock and trade, my play veers from Chikamatsu's model in important ways. Most obviously, it is comic in nature and introduces a play within a play (the creative entourage making a film about the love suicides).

The circumstances of the play and its characters lent themselves to the form of a "screwball comedy." This cinematic genre that began in the aftermath of the Great Depression draws its name from a pitch in baseball that moves in unexpected directions. The play finds its movement through unexpected farcical situations and fast-paced repartee. The genre is noted for its scenes of courtship that satirize traditional love, a female lead who dominates the relationship, and especially for the highly charged verbal interplay that substitutes for sexual activity. These films often include the presence of an out-of-place, improbable hero who tries to outwit others to get his way and usually draws attention to themes that satirize some of the ills of society.

In addition, *The Love Suicides at Takayama* is set in the 1980s, which is more than 250 years after Chikamatsu. The modern characters are better educated, more self-aware, and more cosmopolitan than the characters of the bunraku theatre who focus on a consuming love affair, their day-to-day responsibilities, and issues of survival. I also reinvented the type of falling action in the *Shinjū* to make it more deeply rooted in the psychology of the couple rather than an inevitable direction caused by circumstances.

This turns the tragedy into a bittersweet comedy that speaks directly to a modern audience.

I invite readers to enjoy a style of storytelling that merges aspects of comedic cinema with techniques from the poetic ritual drama of the Japanese puppet theatre established in the 17th century.

Ultimately, this presents a world where partners constrained by society find the freedom to fully know each other as they take their lives (or, rather, in this modern version, take ownership of their lives) and find their own rebirth.

As this work goes to press, I am aware that this is both a literary and a dramatic project that will be published before it is produced. I recognize that there is much more that I can do with this material to expand its strengths and address its limitations for the stage.

I welcome the opportunity to work with a theatre company and its artists— especially directors and actors—to deepen the conflict and characterization to maximize its dramatic potential. It is my hope to see an enhanced version of this work performed in American and Japanese theatres.

Sheppard Ranbom
Washington, DC
September 2025

Act I

Scene 1: At Nagoya Station

NARRATOR

Ah youth. Can you remember a time when you thought you could live on passion as poor artists thrive on dreams and winkles? You probably thought you could bend the future to your will or that any difficulty— even the most restrictive customs and taboos of forbidden love—can be surmountable. This was the case with the playwright Daniel Singer, consumed with desire for the artist Kimiko, his tormentor and muse.... Here he is at 30, still wondering how he will liberate Kimiko and capture his prize. Unable to achieve what he most desires, he reminds us of what the philosopher once said of impotent men. Admit the infirmity and be open to it to ease the constriction.

> *Daniel stands outside a phone booth in the Nagoya Station underground, that beige-tiled underworld of corridors, stores and restaurants. He holds small change in hand, gathering his thoughts. He enters the booth and dials Kimiko's family home.*

KIMIKO

Moshi moshi.

DANIEL

Kimiko-chan, is that you?

KIMIKO

Daniel?

DANIEL

I've missed you. And soon I'll fly back to America.

KIMIKO

You sound like you're in a tunnel.

DANIEL
I'm ready to board the Takayama Express. I can be with you in an hour.

KIMIKO
(*Her voice quavers as if Daniel is holding a knife to her throat.*)
No, don't come, I beg you. By the first stop, my father will find out.
His detectives are on the lookout. He knows we were together
last week. If you so much as set foot in Hida, he will take it out on me.
Daniel, my joy, my curse. What will I do with you? You are oblivious
to our customs and a fool to have wasted your youth on me.
I don't have enough strength to continue this battle with my father.
His bonds are even stronger than your willfulness. He is ready
to choose any suitor other than the man who litters his house
with aerogrammes—the pale-blue paper with writing in a foreign hand.

DANIEL
Kimiko-chan. No one deserves to carry the weight of your obligation—a
life's sentence. Shall we poison ourselves like the acolyte and the
merchant's daughter at the Woman's Temple?

JAPANESE RAILWAY RECORDING
ネストトレインは高山への特急で、トラック4に出発
Nesutotorein wa Takayama e no tokkyū de, Torakku 4 ni shuppatsu

DANIEL
They've just announced the Hida Limited to Takayama.

KIMIKO
I can't talk now. My father is in the next room, and I'm too tired. Send me
a note. I love your letters. Reading them allows me time to translate and
respond.

DANIEL
I'm not far away, but these mountains that you put up between us are
impassable.

NARRATOR
In Nagoya Station, you can hear the click-clack and clatter of heels on the
floor tiles, the *irasshai, irasshai* come-ons of the shopkeepers; the musical
pachi pachi ping of the pachinko balls on the pins; the hyper pitch of high
school students moving in packs. Everyone seems to have places to go....

NARRATOR (Cont.)

But Daniel has no place in mind, and no one is waiting. He wants to send Kimiko books and keepsakes but has second thoughts about how they would be received.

> *Daniel sits on a quiet bench near the telephone. He is hungry but has no appetite. Once more beaten down, all he can do is gnaw at his own circumstance like an animal with a wound.*
>
> *Daniel rises to leave. A foreigner who would try to live here but cannot blend in, he is the only one in the swarming crowd who is visible. He feels as if he is a steel pinball bouncing against the wall of the arcade game.*
>
> *The cast dressed in silver with round hoods, is choreographed to move in a pack. At first, they constantly brush against Daniel and push him backwards. The swarming crowd seems to have a clear path around the stage but Daniel, dressed in jeans and a tee-shirt, bounces off the crowd and the walls. He constantly loses balance, falling and rising. Lights of every color sweep across the stage. The sound of balls hitting the pins set off the reactive noises of a pachinko game.*

NARRATOR

This is the crush of commuter traffic at sundown.

Clueless to signals and cues, Daniel steps into the rushing crowd, bouncing off the station walls and commuters, moving like a pinball dropped through a chute.

See Daniel go knockabout. Foreigners in Japan have long known the nation's indifference and this feeling of loneliness and dislocation.

In premodern times, the shoguns kept Japan isolated. By the 19th century, the only outsiders entering Japan were priests and traders before American sailors broke into Edo Harbor aboard Commodore Perry's gunships.

Daniel wants to be welcomed like a Commodore but lacks a navy to inspire such friendship.

NARRATOR (Cont.)

Detectives are on his tail, seeking any excuse to ship him, pachi pachi, in a crate from Yokohama to Baltimore.

Scene 2: 'Art for the 80s'

NARRATOR

Memory is a bond that holds people together. And the memory of first
love, no matter how many years pass or how much the world may beat us
down, is a reminder of what is deepest in ourselves—the promise of life
in full within our own bloom. Sitting in the station, Daniel remembers
the first time he met Kimiko—at a nursing home in Manhattan where
Daniel's landlady, Mrs. Rubinowicz, was in Kimiko's *'Art for the 80s'* class.

> *Nursing home rec room. Only two people are in the room.*
> *Daniel, at a far-off corner whispering in the dark to the seat*
> *next to him. The spotlight is on Kimiko wearing a pale blue dress*
> *with a kimono pattern sewn in. She makes her way around the*
> *room talking to the residents, providing encouragement as she looks*
> *at their work. She is in her element, serving older people, talking*
> *about art, making personal connections that give the residents what*
> *they need—not a lesson in how to paint or draw or perfect their*
> *work—but a means to share what they cherish.*

KIMIKO

That's great, Mrs. Silverstein. Is this a special place for you?... Tell me
what you remember... I can almost hear the frogs by the lake. The water
is clear and refreshing. Do you like to swim?... Just do it. We'll be your
lifeguards.
> (*Kimiko walks to the next seat and leans over.*)

How does this drawing make you feel?... Don't worry about technique.
All that matters is how alive you feel.... Really? I could use some of that!
> (*She meets the next student who doesn't remember*
> *what class she is in.*)

"I'm here to work with you. Every Thursday morning. Mrs. Nadler. Can
you take out the colored pencils? Did you ever do this in school, maybe
with crayons? What's your favorite color? Excellent. Of course, they still
make it.
> (*Kimiko turns her face to the next seat and smiles.*)

I think, Mr. Gastone, we could use a nude model. Are you volunteering?
No, you might catch cold, and I'd catch hell if you came down with
something.... Tell you what, maybe we could ask that boy over there if he
would pose for us.

Smiles at Daniel. A spotlight sweeps over Daniel, who shakes as if startled at being awakened. He is dressed in white trousers and a white shirt that make him look like an orderly in a hospital or a student with little cash.

KIMIKO

Hello, Mr. Singer. Mrs. Rabinowitcz has told me about you. I know all the great works of literature that you have yet to write. You are what we call a young man of promise, which is a difficult thing to live up to...

DANIEL

I'm just a second-year student at Columbia.

KIMIKO

What are you studying?

DANIEL

The humanities.

KIMIKO

What's that?

DANIEL

It's what makes us human. It begins with language and ends with loss, but I've had limited experience.

KIMIKO

Do you have to do a lot of writing in your area of study?

DANIEL

De-composition mostly. We break down books until the writing is dead... Your English is excellent.

KIMIKO

I studied after school with a native speaker, and I met American college students in Kyoto. But I still must look up many words.

DANIEL

What brings you here? Is this your dream—to teach people to remember?

KIMIKO

I'm a painter. My teacher is a well-known conceptual artist in Japan. He said that I could not be an artist if I didn't experience New York. So he helped me get a fellowship at Parson's and this teaching job, because you can't make a living strictly as an artist.

DANIEL

Well, you seem to be a good teacher. You connect with everyone. Do you give private lessons?

KIMIKO

You're pretty cheeky for such a young man. Are you chatting me up? You seem too young for me.

DANIEL

I'm 19, going on 20. By the looks of it, you could be my older sister. You want to go out for coffee when you're done?

KIMIKO

I have another job after this.

DANIEL

What about Saturday?

KIMIKO

I'm free at noon.

DANIEL

Maybe we could have lunch. What kind of food do you like?

KIMIKO

Do you know a good noodle shop?

DANIEL

I know just the place.

KIMIKO

We can meet here.

DANIEL

Bring a sketch pad. You can sketch my hands. Some say they're my best feature.

KIMIKO

You are very sure of yourself.

DANIEL

I'm very sure of you.

KIMIKO

See you on Saturday.

Scene 3: At the Kugel King

An empty table at the Kugel King, a Jewish specialty shop. It's a help-yourself place. Daniel, wearing his white hospital pants and a purple shirt with thin green stripes and brown shoes, carries a tray with five kinds of kugel and a big bowl of chicken noodle soup. Kimiko, wearing a denim top and skirt, a stylish scarf, and plastic sandals, carries a large pocketbook on one shoulder and a tray with large cups of iced tea. They sit down at the table.

KIMIKO

When I said a noodle shop I meant a Japanese restaurant that serves ramen or udon noodles.

DANIEL

We'll do the Japanese another time.
(*Enthusiastically*)
This place is a real find. Did you see—there's 10 types of kugel—some savory, some sweet. Someday I'll order them all. I generally stick to the *lokshen* kugel, but I wanted to try the mushroom stroganoff. You'll have to tell me how the chicken soup compares with the ramen that you like so much.

KIMIKO

What is kugel?

DANIEL

It's basically a noodle casserole.

KIMIKO

(Poking at the kugel with a fork.)
It's really dense. The noodles are tightly wound.

DANIEL

The Kugel King's slogan is *"More noodles per square foot."*

KIMIKO

(Takes a few bites.)
It's really good... Did you seriously think that this was the kind of noodle shop I was talking about?

9

DANIEL

I wanted to mix things up. It makes for a fun date.

KIMIKO

Is this a date?

DANIEL

Call it what you want. You can start sketching anytime. Any part of me—visible or imagined—is fair game.

KIMIKO

Where on earth did you get that shirt?

DANIEL

I wanted to make an impression.

KIMIKO

(Makes a sour face.)

DANIEL

I guess I did after all.

KIMIKO

My impression is that you never had sisters or a girlfriend to give you fashion advice, and that nobody ever spent a dime on your clothes.

DANIEL

Every penny goes to secondhand books.

KIMIKO

We'll have to find a secondhand clothes shop. You will never wear that shirt again. Promise?

DANIEL

Sure.

KIMIKO

In my country a thousand years ago, a woman wrote the first novel in history. Her name was Lady Muraskai. The novel: *The Tale of Genji*. Genji was known as the Shining Prince. He was famous for his way with the ladies, the beauty of his clothes, and his fine scent. In those days courtiers were judged by how they smelled and by the poems they wrote.

DANIEL

The poetry comes naturally. I'll have to work on the rest.

(*They continue to eat the kugel and the soup.*)

(*Daniel raises his hand sheepishly to ask a question.*)
I want to ask you something. Would it be too forward if I asked how you pronounce your name?

KIMIKO

Kim'-i-ko The accent is on the first syllable.

DANIEL

Kimiko. What is your family name? Does it have any special meaning?

KIMIKO

The surname is Miyagawa. It is a river and a village in the prefecture where I was born.

DANIEL

That's impressive. My ancestors took the name of the sewing machine that gave them their livelihood.

Kimiko becomes very sweet towards him. She cuts up bits of kugel and puts it on his plate. Daniel is thrilled with the attention.

Let's talk about things that you do know. Tell me about school. What are your favorite courses? Who are your professors?

Kimiko takes out her sketchbook and begins to draw him. They talk enthusiastically back and forth, Kimiko asking questions, Daniel taking more kugel for his plate.

Scene 4: Private Lessons

NARRATOR

They start to meet each other regularly in Asian noodle restaurants and coffee shops. They often pass the hours in Kimiko's apartment, listening to classical music while she sketches and he studies. Daniel, a scholarship student who does not have a job, is too poor to explore the city. When they go to jazz clubs and movies or expensive restaurants, she is happy to treat him.

At Kimiko's apartment. It is a small efficiency where the practical things of life—a rice cooker and an ironing board are mixed with her artwork, easel, and a small upright piano. A bust of Plato is on the wall where her own watercolors of the residents of the nursing home are displayed.

They sit around a kotatsu, a small table on the floor that is equipped with a heater, to keep their legs warm. They sit on pillows on the floor, studying each other, writing notes back and forth. She occasionally looks up words in her dictionary.

KIMIKO

I think you must learn Japanese. I shouldn't be the only one who has to use a dictionary.

DANIEL

Why don't we start now. I want to know the words for everything in this room, so I'll never forget them.

KIMIKO

Okay.

DANIEL

How do you say 'apartment'?

KIMIKO

Aparto.

DANIEL

Aparto. How do you say 'Kimiko's apartment'?

KIMIKO

Kimiko no aparto.

DANIEL

Kimiko no aparto.
     (Pointing at the paintings on the wall.)
'Watercolor painting.'

KIMIKO

Suisaiga.

DANIEL

Suisaiga. Okay. How about 'rice cooker'?

KIMIKO

Suihanki.

DANIEL

Suihanki. How do you say 'Plato's head'?

KIMIKO

Plato no atama.

DANIEL

Plato no atama. 'Nose.'

KIMIKO

Hana.

DANIEL

Hana. 'Kimiko's nose.'

KIMIKO

Kimiko no hana.

DANIEL

Kimiko no hana. Okay. Now teach me a sentence. 'I touch Kimiko's nose.'

KIMIKO

Watashi wa Kimiko no hana ni fure masu.

DANIEL

Watashi wa Kimiko no hana ni fure masu. Okay. How do you say 'face.'

KIMIKO

Kao.

DANIEL

Kao.
> *(Touching her face)*

Lips.

KIMIKO

Kuchibiru.

DANIEL

Kiss.

KIMIKO

Kisu.

DANIEL
> *(Kisses Kimiko, who responds unhesitatingly, then after a time pulls away.)*

Watashi wa Kimiko no kuchibiru ni kisu wa shi masu. [I kiss Kimiko's lips.]

KIMIKO

I'm the teacher. I run the class.

DANIEL

Am I your favorite student?

KIMIKO

I like staring at you. You're cute and funny.

DANIEL

Okay. You can draw my hands again. He puts his arms around her and holds her close to him, kissing her hair.

KIMIKO

How am I supposed to draw if you hold me?

DANIEL

You don't have to draw anything. How do you say, 'This is all I need in the world'?

KIMIKO

This is all I want in the world....

DANIEL

Okay. No more talking.
(*Kisses her again.*)

Scene 5: Reunion with the director

NARRATOR

Daniel has extracted himself from the crowded station and from his daydreams. He has arranged to meet Nomura, the film director. Now free to move at will, he walks the streets at dusk, inventing the names of streets and landmarks. Walking along the Quiet Street of Dusk, and beyond, to the red-light district with its own Ferris Wheel, Quick Eats, and Bicycle Alley, and Sex Den Boulevard underneath the TV tower. He hails a cab to the bar near the Stonewall House of the Camelia Trees.

The jazz club is decorated with photos and displays of horn players. On the walls of the tokonoma are Miles Davis's leopard skin shawl, Dizzy Gillespie's red mute, and Clifford Brown's fuzzy fedora. The music is quiet and soothing. Daniel and Nomura eat grilled octopus and drink whiskey from heavy glass tumblers.

NOMURA

The last time we met I was your interpreter in Tokyo.

DANIEL

You were a godsend. You opened many doors.

NOMURA

What brings you here today?

DANIEL

I wanted to surprise my girlfriend in Takayama, but I only reached Nagoya Station. The possibility that I would meet her family was so overwhelming for her, you'd think it would cause an international incident. Like General Ripper and the nuclear codes.

NOMURA

How often do you see her?

DANIEL

We have had a rendezvous in Kyoto or Tokyo every year since we met. In past years we said we were going to visit college friends. Now her friends are married with children and our plans have become more complex. We've grown tired of sneaking around.

NOMURA

You've been together so long, breaking it off after a dozen years might seem hasty. Let me raise my glass and offer a toast. Here's to the trifecta— your belief in yourself, your tenacity, and your foolishness. You know, in the old days you could buy the courtesan's freedom from the innkeeper. But in this case, the keeper is her father. So, what's your plan? Will you show up anyway?

DANIEL

I don't know.

NOMURA

You could find a new girlfriend.

DANIEL

That's not an option.

NOMURA

Why not?

DANIEL

My feelings for her are sincere.

NOMURA

If you storm the house, you'll lose her.

DANIEL

I could use your help again. When we last met, you suggested that I write a screenplay about this fine mess.

NOMURA

It could find a wide audience. People want a good love story.

DANIEL

I'd like to write a treatment for you.

NOMURA

Well, you know the material better than anyone. The challenge will be exposing all your flaws, looking at the hard, imperfect stone of character and flipping over the rock to see what crawls underneath.

DANIEL

I'm moving into a new medium. Writing for the stage is a matter of dramatic compression. Film is a wide-open canvas.

NOMURA

I'm between projects and can help you get through.

DANIEL

I'll need some cash to tide me over.

NOMURA

How much?

DANIEL

Three thousand dollars up front. I'll also need help extending my visa.

NOMURA

I'll sponsor you.

DANIEL

There is one more thing.

NOMURA

You can't be shy in this business. What is it?

DANIEL

I want final say on the script.

NOMURA

(*Laughs.*)
You are asking a lot for a novice.

DANIEL

I can do this.

NOMURA

You may write like Chikamatsu, but we'll need Billy Wilder or Dalton Trumbo. Besides, how will I know this isn't going to be another 12-year production?

DANIEL

I'm productive at work.

NOMURA

I started my own company, because I wanted complete control of the work process, not to give it away. Besides, it is in your interest that I have my stamp on the project. You've seen my work. And the story needs to work for both of us. We can be 50-50 partners. What I have in mind is a mashup of David Lean's *Summertime*—the sudden romance that has to end—and William Wyler's *Roman Holiday*. Show the father's private detectives—not the paparazzi—run you and the girl around Kyoto. What's funny to me is that, in the *Summertime* part, I see you as the demure one. Kimiko has her way with you.

DANIEL

We'll need to go on location to her village.

NOMURA

Leave the arrangements to me. I want you to write your heart out. Imagine you're listening to the soundtrack of *Dr. Zhivago*. The revolution is over. A new world awaits… I hope you don't mind me assigning one of my producers to work closely with you. You may know her. She's an actress. Velva, Velva Ogata. She can help with research, logistics, and dialogue.

DANIEL

I won't need help with dialogue.

NOMURA

I want you to work with a real woman, not some idealized figure in your head. And Velva is a real woman, I can assure you.

DANIEL

Are you suggesting I wouldn't know what a real woman is like?

NOMURA

Consider it another investment in your development as a screenwriter.

DANIEL

Where did she get the name Velva?

NOMURA

Her family is very conservative. They run a textile factory and a kimono shop in Nagoya. But she had a great aunt who at the turn of the century was a friend of Sarah Bernhardt and performed at the Odéon in Paris and the Coliseum in London. Velva was the woman's stage name. The family gives young Velva great latitude, because she inherited talent with languages and the performance gene.

DANIEL

Do we have a deal?

NOMURA

You'll have a standard contract and cash tomorrow.

(*Nomura and Daniel shake hands.*)

Scene 6: Testing the treatment

Three weeks later, Daniel has submitted his treatment for review. He comes to Nomura's office and is eager to hear the director's reaction. It is a small suite like any talent agency in New York, London, or Tokyo with stills from famous films. Mixed in are also posters from Nomura's movies. Velva sits across from Daniel at a table in the conference room. He stares through the glass window beyond her.

VELVA
If you're expecting Mr. Nomura, he's not coming. He gives me free reign.

DANIEL
I am trying to remember the roles you've played. Weren't you the jilted nurse in *When I Whistle* and the daughter-in-law in *The Sound of the Mountain?*

VELVA
That's right. And Nomura has told me about you.

DANIEL
No doubt.

VELVA
He says you may have a few writing ticks suitable only for the stage. You might be too scholarly, which is poison to a film audience.

DANIEL
Thanks for being honest.

VELVA
We have to be straight with each other to be any good.

DANIEL
Let's keep it that way.

VELVA
You know, Nomura collects people he likes. Consider it a compliment to be one of them.

DANIEL

How did he find you?

VELVA

I took his history of film class. He liked the fact that I spoke French and English and wanted to be an actress.

DANIEL

Did you start right away in his films?

VELVA

I was his go-fer and technical assistant. I screened foreign films for ideas that he could borrow. It was tedious, but he raised precise questions, which helped me learn.

DANIEL

So you'll show me how to shift from bunraku to the big screen?

VELVA

Yes.

DANIEL

Make any changes you want, as long as they don't cheapen the script. What do you think of the direction so far?

VELVA

I like the story, the characters, and the banter. But there are three problems that we have to work out. First, film has to work for the eye. You need to develop a visual logic and language. Second, the treatment is too résigné. The focus is on the insurmountable problem—what *can't* happen, while there is not enough happening. Third, the girlfriend has too much power and that strains the relationship. They seem like a couple who met through an arranged marriage proposal rather than passionate people who found each other. The man and the woman have their own emotions *away from each other*. We want their feelings to cook in the same pot and boil over onscreen.

DANIEL

What are we shooting for, exactly?

VELVA

Take the goodbye scene at the confectionary shop when he must go back to New York. Their feelings are buried inside themselves. The couple seem paralyzed. Where's the passion and the disappointment? When I read it, it seemed like it would be a relief for Kimiko to let you go. I'd want you to go myself. It's not so attractive to see you tie yourself in knots. Let's play that scene.

(Both stand up facing each other at a protective distance.)
You've got your luggage. Now, say what you want to say.

DANIEL

I want to stay with you. But I don't know how to make that happen. My visa is expiring, and I still have to finish college.

VELVA

(Laughs)
Let's not let the facts get in the way. Imagine you are the same age and you've quit school to be with her. You're fluent in Japanese. You can do what you want. Look me in the eye and tell me what you would tell her.

DANIEL

All I want is to be with you. Why can't we be together?

VELVA

You are giving all your power away. Speak as if the answer lies inside you.

DANIEL

Okay.
(Takes a breath and tries again with more passion)
We have nothing to live for but each other. You and I have no barriers between us.

VELVA

Better. Now hold me and build on that.

DANIEL

(Approaches Velva with some caution and gently holds her to him.)
We have nothing to live for but each other. There are no more barriers. To leave you now would be like death, and we're only beginning to live. My desire to live is too great to say goodbye.

Velva leans forward and kisses him. It is the kind of kiss that is trying to explore who he is and what he is made of. She waits for his response. He kisses her back, the goodbye a kind of welcome, raising more questions as they linger, until she pulls away.

DANIEL

What was that?

VELVA

That's how you meet—or say goodbye—in film. It was really nice. And it doesn't cheapen anything.

Scene 7: The stalemated lovers and their entourage in the underground

Return to the underground at Nagoya Station. Daniel feels more confident when he meets Kimiko this time. They meet at the station and—as planned—pretend not to know each other. He walks by her. She follows at a distance and enters the same ramen shop where they sit together.

DANIEL

What did you tell the Colonel?

KIMIKO

I told him I needed art supplies.

DANIEL

How long do we have?

KIMIKO

Till the five o'clock train.

DANIEL

Come with me. Let's not waste a minute.
    (*They enter the restaurant and take seats.*)

DANIEL

Remember when we went to the karaoke bar and you sang "Imagine" with your own lyrics.

KIMIKO

That's my theme song.
    (*Sings.*)
Imagine there's no parents.
It isn't hard to do.
No family obligations.
No children, too.

DANIEL

    (*Laughing*)
I love that song.

KIMIKO

If only we could change reality to our liking!

DANIEL

Of course we can! What would you change?

KIMIKO

Takao, my oldest brother, would still be alive. And the next oldest would not have married and taken another family's name. I would be free. I'd have no responsibility to continue the family line.

DANIEL

Your father had his life and now he wants yours. You give him your attention and devotion. But he wants grandchildren, and you're not ready, and the time is running short. So what does he gain? It's a stalemate.

KIMIKO

(*Scolding*)
We don't live only to please ourselves. We are ruled by *giri*, our responsibilities to others....

DANIEL

What did we do in our previous lives to deserve this?

KIMIKO

(*Laughing*)
We were probably married. You were a shit husband and a worse father. It was a big mistake.

DANIEL

And now—according to the Buddhist way—I must repent by being a nonperson in this life? All I can do is kill us off in the script or go to your house and wreck the furniture. The worst part is doing nothing.

KIMIKO

We're together now, aren't we?

DANIEL

I'm not sure. Is there anyone that you're serious about? It's enough that I have your father for a rival.

KIMIKO

Yes, there is someone. He's not that handsome, but he's very sure of himself. The downside is that he is younger than I am and an alien.

DANIEL

If I came to Takayama, would you pretend not to know me?

KIMIKO

I'd pretend that you were an alien who wanted to abduct me.

DANIEL

We shouldn't treat this situation lightly. We are like the two stars at the opposite end of the galaxy—the hunter boy and the weaver girl who meet once a year when the birds make a bridge across the heavens.

KIMIKO

Not even the birds can bring us together. We're mismatched. Not soulmates. Stalemates.

DANIEL

I don't give up easily. A playwright creates problems in the first act to be resolved by the third.

KIMIKO

The curtain should have fallen on us a long time ago.

DANIEL

If I were a mystery writer, I would get rid of your father. Feed him poison blowfish that I prepared myself.
    (*Laughing to himself.*)
Feed him the sweetest American chocolates that would put him in a diabetic coma.... What if we commit love suicide on his front steps. Would that change his mind?

KIMIKO

Yes. But where would that leave us?

DANIEL

In a better place.

KIMIKO

If we can't be together, I'm glad that you can write about us. At least I can advance your career.

DANIEL

I'd rather have you than a film career.

KIMIKO

And what would we live on?

DANIEL

I can write for magazines back home. Or make connections in Japanese theatre or international TV. If you just wanted to be a pajama girl, you could spend your days in a housedress.

KIMIKO

So instead of being obligated to my father, I'll be obligated to you?

DANIEL

It wouldn't be an obligation.

KIMIKO

Dah-meh. I have to be my own person.

DANIEL

All right. How's this for a modern solution? He can make a test tube baby from his own sperm. You can have another Miyagawa—the crown prince—to carry on the family.

KIMIKO

He wouldn't like that idea. He doesn't believe in GMOs.

DANIEL

Your father is a larger figure in your life than me, and he's much needier. Which seems impossible.

KIMIKO

Because you are so needy?

DANIEL

Yes. So tell me you want me to take you away, and not just for a weekend.

KIMIKO

I want you—Mr. Hideous Alien—to take me away.... for a few hours.

DANIEL

I'll follow you home. I'll arrive at your doorstep as the pizza delivery man.

KIMIKO

My father likes anchovies, my mother veggies, and I just like the delivery man.

DANIEL

(*A satisfied smile.*)
Now that's more like it.... In the rare moments when you are not thinking of me, what goes on at home?

KIMIKO

I paint forbidden American landscapes from memory. And I've been sketching my father. I'm making a statue of him in the manner of St. Gaudens.

DANIEL

Will you make him a hero on horseback? Or a Puritan who flogs his congregation?

KIMIKO

He will be my own founding father. His life is exemplary to everyone but me. He keeps setting up these meetings. One suitor had four children. Another was a highway engineer whose idea of a good time was a drive on the turnpike to Nagano. The best prospect is one of the private detectives who follows us.

DANIEL

What does he look like?

KIMIKO

You know him. It's Kareshi. The guy you call my boyfriend. He chased us around Kyoto. See him in the corner reading the paper?...

DANIEL

Not him again. He keeps coming back. It's my worst nightmare.

KIMIKO

Tell me more about this actress you run around with?

DANIEL

Who, Velva?

KIMIKO

What kind of name is Velva?

DANIEL

It's like any other name, only sexier.

KIMIKO

What's she like?

DANIEL

She's a lot of things you're not.

KIMIKO

Like what?

DANIEL

For one thing, she's been naked on stage. She has no concern about showing affection—or anything else—in public. She's helping me with the script.

KIMIKO

And how is that going?

DANIEL

You'll have to ask her. She'll be here any minute.

KIMIKO

Maybe we can set her up with the detective.

DANIEL

I don't know. He seems more interested in me.

KIMIKO

He has a crush on you, for sure. He won't stop until he kisses you goodbye.... And how did you meet Nomura, the director?

DANIEL

Through the Embassy. He was my guide and interpreter. He knows all about you. He thinks you must be exceptional, because I've never given up on you. Have you seen his films?

KIMIKO

I looked him up. I know *Do-des-ka-den*, Not the ones he's made on his own.

DANIEL

His most recent film was an adaptation of Endo's *When I Whistle*.

KIMIKO

Oh, I saw that. The old man was spectacular.

DANIEL

If I write a good part for your father, would he change his attitude?

KIMIKO

He hates flattery. And he doesn't care what people think about him. He's very honest that way.

> *Daniel brightens when Kimiko holds his hand under the table.*
> *Nomura, in a grey business suit and black oxfords enters with*
> *Velva, who wears a fringed, sequined shoulder dress with a green-*
> *tinted, studded, feathered headband like a flapper; only her hair*
> *doesn't need the feather; it stands up on its own.*

DANIEL

The great man himself and the lovely Miss Velva. This is Miss Miyagawa.

NOMURA

(*Bows to Kimiko and gives her his business card.*)
You know, I didn't know you were real. Daniel said you were funny, talented, and a great beauty. I can guess about the first two qualities, but I can attest to the last.

VELVA

What am I, the brains of this outfit?

NOMURA

No. But it's quite an outfit.

DANIEL

Stunning. I was talking with Kimiko-san about your performance in *When I Whistle*.

KIMIKO

When the doctor dumped you, the whole audience hissed as if they were watching a silent movie.

DANIEL

Does the old man in the film resemble your father?

KIMIKO

Nothing like him. He's more like Sessue Hayakawa in *Bridge over the River Kwai*.

DANIEL

So he's hardened and cold. Sadistic?

KIMIKO

You never let up.

VELVA

(*Squeezing his arm.*)

Daniel, you are very convincing as the neglected lover. The desperate look, the snide commentary. When you finally break down, I'll come to your rescue. I'll be the nurse who brings you back to life.

KIMIKO

He's convincing for an alien.

NOMURA

Did Daniel tell you the real purpose of our meeting?

KIMIKO

He's writing a movie about our relationship.

DANIEL

I'm a script doctor. I write scripts that need doctoring.

NOMURA

We're planning to visit Takayama to scout locations. We'd love to see your house and meet your parents, too.

DANIEL
(*With a false accent*).
I could come as Sergei Ivanovich, the Russian cinematographer.

KIMIKO
He already knows what you look like.

DANIEL
(*Turning his head to the detective.*)
Well, now he knows what we all look like. There's a detective watching us.

VELVA
Which one?

DANIEL
The one at the counter doing the fan dance behind the newspaper.

KIMIKO
He's actually quite attractive.

Kimiko delivers Nomura's business card to the detective. She flirts with him, laughing and smiling, which makes Daniel uncomfortable. She returns to the filmmaker's table, leading Kareshi by the hand.

KIMIKO
Let me introduce you. This is Mr. Kareshi. Our friends here are well known in the movie industry. Mr. Nomura is a director who worked with Kurosawa. Miss Velva Ogawa is a rising star. The ugly American, Mr. Singer, hopes to become Velva's boyfriend.

DANIEL
I'm so glad to be reacquainted. I prefer to have you join us rather than chase us at high speeds through narrow streets.

KIMIKO
We risked our lives on rides to nowhere.

KARESHI
You weren't in danger.

DANIEL

Can you even be objective? Your feelings for Kimiko affect your judgment.

KARESHI

I won't testify against myself. For me, any kind of investigation and police work is second nature. I don't take it personally. But keeping tabs on Kimiko is a different story.

DANIEL

So why do you do it?

KARESHI

It's the only way I get to see her.

DANIEL

Doesn't it strike you as unnatural?

KARESHI

Not until you are out of the picture.

DANIEL

Kim-chan, can you set up a visit to your house? We'd like to scout locations.

KIMIKO

(To Kareshi)

Tell my father that the creative team behind a new project, *The Love Suicides at Takayama*, will come for a day to see us and the old village.... Why don't you join us for a drink? We can take group photos to send home with you.

> *The stage and audience are blinded by repeated flashes of Kareshi's camera taking group shots, during which Velva kisses Daniel again. The room lights up like magnesium lit with a Bunsen burner.*

Act II

Scene 1: Up in the clouds

In a Bentley, Nomura drives with Velva beside him. Daniel is seated in the back. The backdrop, perhaps on easily moveable clothes racks, includes blown-up photos of a river, the peak of Mt. Ontake. and the city of Takayama, the high ground of Japan.

VELVA

We are up in the clouds. You can see Mount Ontake and Takayama in the distance.

NOMURA

Many Chinese poets and sages who have influenced Japanese culture have lived at this altitude. Their wisdom and weirdness may have been caused by the thin air in the mountains. They say that the poet Li Ling was a heavy drinker. He liked to walk in the nude. He'd tell his visitors: "I see the earth and sky as my home, and this room as my pants. What are you, gentlemen, doing in my pants?"

DANIEL
(*Defensively.*)
Now look here, I'm not trying to get in anybody's pants…. I simply want to see how Kimiko lives and win over her father.

NOMURA

That's what we're here for.

DANIEL

He'll be hard to budge. Miyagawa was a war hero. A squadron commander in World War II. Today he is something of a lightning rod for environmental causes. He runs the agricultural research station in Takayama. He persuaded the farmers to use organic methods when it was all the rage to overuse pesticides and fertilizer. His stubbornness is probably the reason the rivers in Hida are the cleanest in Japan.

NOMURA

Let's give Miyagawa a wide berth. It's going to be just tea with friends.
Try to avoid conflict. Daniel should barely look in Kimiko's direction. I'll
enter first. Velva, you keep the conversation moving. Daniel, take your
cues from Velva and me. She can translate.

VELVA

And I can set up the ring for a Sumo match.

DANIEL

Her father is not my enemy.

VELVA

It's all one package. Love the house, love its crow.

NOMURA

She's great with the ad lib. She'll steal any scene.

VELVA

I have to. My parts are so small.

DANIEL

(*Scans her body.*)
Nothing wanting there.

NOMURA

(*Leaning back to talk to Daniel.*)
She'd prefer a leading role than character work. It's the oldest story in the
business.

VELVA

(*Pouts*)
What's the problem?
(*Batting her eyelashes.*)
I'm not glamorous?

NOMURA

You're the type of actress people want to see more of…. So we keep them
wanting more.

VELVA

All right. You've pegged me as the dull brooch, not the shiny diamond. Every actress at some point has to wear tarnished jewelry.

NOMURA

Daniel, what can you tell us about Kareshi?

DANIEL

He's a private dick. Let me correct that. He's just a dick. He's Miyagawa's pet gorilla. He enjoys trying to intimidate me. His friends on the police force tried to take away my visa. Now he's hitting on Kimiko.

VELVA

How does that work?

DANIEL

I have no idea. But it tells you what her father thinks of me. He considers the detective who taps his daughter's phone a better suitor. You can't make this up.

NOMURA

Look at it from his perspective. If you take Kimiko to America, who's going to care for him in his dotage?

DANIEL

If he can hire a detective, he can hire a caregiver.

VELVA

Maybe he'll warm up to you.

NOMURA

Let's not get too far ahead of ourselves.

VELVA

Speaking of getting ahead, do I have to play myself in the movie? I'd like to read for Kimiko's part.

NOMURA

(Laughs.)
You're never satisfied. I could cast you as Kimiko's mother.

VELVA

You may have discovered me, but you're still a poor judge of talent.

NOMURA

I'm trying to show you that every part is important. You'll have to deal with that. One day you will take over our company and make these tough decisions yourself.

VELVA

(*Stunned*)

That's funny. I've always worked as if I could get the axe tomorrow.

NOMURA

I could hardly cut you out of a scene much less my work.

DANIEL

Velva, what's more important? Top billing or making a great film?

VELVA

All things being equal, I'd prefer to play Kimiko.

NOMURA

The character of Velva would be lost without the real Velva playing the role.

Scene 2: Life with father

The Shoin room of the Miyagawa house in what is now Hida City is a spacious, empty hall with high ceilings, a giant dragon screen in back, traditional sliding doors, and walls of thicker paper. Spread around are plaster reliefs and scale drawings taped to the screens and doors. Kimiko is creating an eight-foot bronze sculpture of her father that will find its place in the village. Kimiko stands on one side of the room.

Miyagawa is posing for her wearing a cloak like that worn by Oda Nobunaga, the great unifier of Japan, and wears a sword in a scabbard. The dignified and imposing lift of his head is spoiled by the fact that he is fidgeting and uncomfortable being the sole focus of his daughter's attention.

KIMIKO
Didn't you learn to stand at attention in the military?

MIYAGAWA
Why don't you just paint my portrait?

KIMIKO
A statue suits you. Only a statue can capture your heft, the mountains that shaped you, and the rust of a bygone age.

MIYAGAWA
My detractors will call me a narcissist. They'll say that I forced you to create a monument to my vanity.

KIMIKO
Who could say a word against you? You've left a handsome legacy. One could argue that an eight-foot statue isn't big enough. I should cast you the size of the Great Buddha of Nara. You are a monument, my father.

MIYAGAWA
(*Chuckling.*)
You are mocking me again. You really are enjoying this, aren't you? I suppose, if you chose, you could shape my buttocks like a barrel and make me look like a turtle-faced, mutant yokai.

KIMIKO
(*Writes as if making a checklist.*)
Let's see…. Bottom of the barrel. Head of a tortoise. I was seeking more
dignity, but if you insist….

MIYAGAWA
This is your chance to get even.

KIMIKO
No. To show you the respect you deserve. Though you like to speak in
edicts, and that's not a language I know, you are a man who takes his
responsibilities seriously. You make sure the birds are fed in winter. The
mute swans have returned.

MIYAGAWA
They are prospering. There are more cygnets this year than ever. The cobs
alone could devour our fields. I've saved the spring *nabana* to feed them.
Why don't you come to take some photos?

KIMIKO
What—to study the male appetite? I worry about being devoured
myself—by your dictums, by the plans you and other men make for me.

MIYAGAWA
You pretend to be a victim. But you have me and everyone else wrapped
around your finger. If only we could talk more and fight less, your time in
Takayama would be bearable.

KIMIKO
You'd be lonely without someone to quarrel with.

MIYAGAWA
I'd rather fight with the American.

KIMIKO
You mean Tokubei, the one I'm never to mention in this house?

MIYAGAWA
That's him. If his name is Daniel and he's American, why do you call him
Tokubei?

KIMIKO

He resembles the lead character in Chikamatsu's plays—the man who must commit suicide to succeed in love.

MIYAGAWA

I'm beginning to feel sorry for him.

KIMIKO

You should. You put him in a tough spot—lost inside the labyrinth of unfulfilled love—a maze that leads towards me but cannot reach me…. There is one thing you can do for me today. At the very least, I expect you to be civil to him. He has suffered, and he needs to know that you are worthy of respect and not simply an obstacle in his quest. Can you do that?

MIYAGAWA

Good manners are as much a part of the samurai code as courage in combat.

KIMIKO

Oh, that awful code that tells us how to live. But for what do we live? So that our ancestors can think well of us? Don't we have an obligation to ourselves?

MIYAGAWA

What's gotten into you, Kim-chan?

KIMIKO

Sumimasen. [I'm sorry.] The American is coming and I must brace myself.

MIYAGAWA

How can I help?

KIMIKO

I remember when Takao and I were children. You taught us to look through a camera. I asked every possible question about how to take pictures: how to use the light, how to get the right background, how to suggest what the picture meant without words…. You never told us how to do it. You said to go out and take a million photographs and make each one different in its own way, and then I would find out how to make the photos stand out. That's what made me an artist and Takao a poet.

MIYAGAWA

I wanted you to see everything.

KIMIKO

So why can't I live my life as freely?

MIYAGAWA

Because I can't bear that you would marry him, and I can't bear to be away from you. Now don't ask any more questions. The guests will arrive soon. I'll change my clothes. We will treat them as if they were emissaries of Lord Oda. I will offer our best sake and pour it myself.

> *A loud commotion outside. The sounds of the car doors closing and the arriving entourage.*

KIMIKO

At ease, Lord Tortoise. They are already here. Let them see you as you are, in the daimyo's battle clothes. I'll make tea and prepare the treats to welcome them.

Scene 3: Tea at the Miyagawas

Mrs. Miyagawa, Kimiko's mother, welcomes the travelers at the door. She is an attractive, fashionable woman in her mid-60s dressed in a white tunic with a cashmere wrap and a knee-length skirt with black tights. Her daughter resembles her in style.

Each guest gives Mrs. Miyagawa a small gift or omiyage—*Nagoya specialties that Velva bought.*

NOMURA

Good morning. We picked out some delicacies from Nagoya.
(*Each hands over a package as they enter—Daniel, ogura; Velva, white chocolate cookies; and Nomura, pickled radish.*)

MRS. MIYAGAWA

How thoughtful. *Ogura*—buttered toast with bean paste—is my favorite. They used to say that Nagoya was most famous for Toyota and the castle, but I think its greatest feature is the confectionary.

KIMIKO

Mother, father, this is Nomura *sensei*, the director. You loved his movies.

NOMURA

Thank you for hosting us.

MIYAGAWA

I am happy to meet this man. Sir, you are an exceptional artist. You understand the codes that we live by.

NOMURA

Thank you. I feel lucky to have grown up in a culture where traditions are valued and audiences appreciate my work.

MIYAGAWA

Compared to the violent movies of American directors, your films may seem unconventional. But what I see is old-fashioned courtesy and a precise attention to detail.

NOMURA

Thank you.

KIMIKO

This is Ms. Ogata. Velva is an actress who works with Mr. Nomura. She is also a producer on the project.

VELVA

Pleased to meet you.

KIMIKO

And this is Daniel Singer, who we call Tokubei. As you know, I first met him when I was studying art and working in New York City.

.

DANIEL
(*Speaking to Mr. and Mrs. Miyagawa.*)
Watashi wa Daniel desu. Dôzo yoroshiku. Onegaishimasu. [Translation: "I am Daniel. Pleased to meet you." Literally, the last phrase means, "Please take care of me."]

MR./MRS. MIYAGAWA

Kochira koso onegaishimasu. [Translation:"The pleasure is all ours."]

MRS. MIYAGAWA
(*Whispers something inaudible to Kimiko.*)

DANIEL

What did she say?

KIMIKO

She said you speak Japanese like John Wayne.

ALL
(*Laughter.*)

NOMURA

And he speaks English like Mifune.

ALL
(*Laughter*)

MRS. MIYAGAWA

(*To the group.*)
Have you had a good trip?

NOMURA

I felt we were riding above the clouds.

VELVA

I just love these *minka* houses. I bet you can see the whole valley from a
side window.

MRS. MIYAGAWA

Yes, but it's a fishbowl. Everyone knows your business.

MIYAGAWA

This house was built by the Shogun's craftsmen as reward for my family's
bravery at Sekigahara. Our history lives with us in the house. It feeds and
nurtures us.

> *They sit beside the hearth. Daniel sits opposite Velva, who is
> dressed conservatively in a blue business suit with a white blouse.
> The house seems simply lit and filled with shadows. The wooden
> floor and walls are warm in the faint glow. Velva's smile and
> vibrant energy give depth to the shadows. On the table are
> assorted fruits from the valley—sliced apples and pears—and a
> Mount Blanc cake. For the occasion, Kimiko has purchased
> lemon blueberry mochi muffins and prepared donuts in the
> shape of swans. The donuts are coated with confectionary sugar.*

MRS. MIYAGAWA

Will everyone have tea?

VELVA

That would be lovely.

DANIEL

Yes. Thanks.

NOMURA

You have gone to much trouble.

Mrs. Miyagawa pours the tea, her husband the sake. The entourage claps their hands and says the Japanese consecration for the gifts received.

ALL

Itadakimasu. [Literally, "I humbly accept" or "For what we are about to take."]

MRS. MIYAGAWA

Kim-chan made the donuts. She shaped them like the silent swans that we're famous for. The Hida Mountains are the only place in Japan where you will find them. There are a few hundred in the mountain lakes and the Miyagawa River.

DANIEL

(His face is white with confectioner's sugar.)
These donuts are fabulous. The more I eat, the more I want.

MIYAGAWA

You have a powerful appetite.

VELVA

He's been on a strict diet. No sugar!

(Daniel puts the food down.)

DANIEL

There's muffins over there.

MIYAGAWA

Daniel-san, I understand you take your Japanese name from the great dramas of old. How did you learn about Chikamatsu?

DANIEL

I look to the past for inspiration. Chikamatsu's tales of samurai, merchants, and courtesans were drawn from newspaper headlines and played by wooden puppets. The puppets come alive for me. They are heroic and capable of joy and suffering.

MIYAGAWA

It was a time of upheaval and clashing social classes. In one play, he insists that the children of merchants are best off marrying the children of merchants, the artisans with the artisans, the samurai with the samurai.

DANIEL

Yes, I know the play, *The Love Suicides at the Woman's Temple*. You can guess my position. I think intermarriage brings the world closer and makes us all smarter and better looking.

NOMURA

(Makes "cut" signal, moving his hand across his throat.)

MIYAGAWA

(Coughs up his sake.)

KIMIKO

(Pours water and offers him a drink.) Are you okay?

MIYAGAWA

Went down the wrong pipe....

VELVA

(Like a talk show host.)
Chohatsu, desu ne? He's provocative, isn't he? Daniel raises important questions. Could we adapt to become a more open society?

DANIEL

Miscegenation will change attitudes faster than if the country opens its borders. The country needs to do both... What do you hate about immigrants? We might carry your daughters off to our Mongolian horde?

MIYAGAWA

Is this man a comedian?
  (Recovers himself.)
You don't give us enough credit. Our people are already smart and good looking. That's something worth preserving, don't you agree?.... (*To Velva.*) You and the American seem close to each other. Are you a couple?

VELVA

We have a great working relationship.

KIMIKO

She's his lifeline. He can't take his eyes off her.

MIYAGAWA

And she covers for him so well....
(*Speaking beneath his breath.*)
Too bad they're not a couple.
(*In a normal tone.*)
What is this movie about?

NOMURA

How lovers—aligned in interest and temperament—find each other, fall for each other, and have to part—because of traditional rules of her culture. It will be a movie full of sorrow and regret, ending in love suicides.

MIYAGAWA

How depressing. Can't he find American women more to his liking?

KIMIKO

Let's ask him.
(*Playfully.*)
Daniel, how many dates have you been on in the last year?

DANIEL

Seven.

KIMIKO

Any prospects?

DANIEL

None. It's hard to find someone who meets my qualifications. Have all fathers taken the most exasperating women off the market?

MIYAGAWA

Only when they drag their feet, unsatisfied with the matches.

MRS. MIYAGAWA

You have us all wondering, Daniel, what you are looking for in a girlfriend.

DANIEL
(*Looking at Mrs. Miyagawa*)
Someone playful and full of laughter. Someone who is artistic and good with language. A firecracker who keeps me honest and focused. Someone like any of the women in this room.

KIMIKO
And someone who wants children?

DANIEL
Not necessarily. One doesn't need to have children to be generative. You can be an artist or a teacher to bring things to life.

KIMIKO
We should take care of each other, whether or not we have children. And I don't think I could bear the pain of losing a child. I've seen what that does.

MIYAGAWA
What has happened in the world that people don't want children?

VELVA
A woman works, raises children, keeps the home, and supports a husband's work.... That's a teeter-totter ready to topple.

NOMURA
I couldn't have had three kids if my wife wasn't willing to sacrifice her career. She left an amazing job—secretary to Prime Minister Nakasone. Now she has no perks. There's nothing glamorous or rewarding about living with me. I'm generally more available when I travel than at home. She says that I live on location.

KIMIKO
(*Looking over the men.*)
So often the man is just another child to take care of.

DANIEL
(*Brightening.*)
Let's change the subject to what we all want to hear: What was Kimiko like as a child?

MIYAGAWA

(*Smiling.*)
She hasn't changed.

DANIEL

So, she was always infuriating?

MIYAGAWA

Let's say 'difficult.'

MRS. MIYAGAWA

She was sensitive.

MIYAGAWA

She struggled to have her way with her brothers and me.

MRS. MIYAGAWA

She was always crying.

DANIEL

Is that possible?

MIYAGAWA

She'd cry when she wanted to go somewhere. When we bought her clothes
or she shopped for clothes. When she went to school. When she watched
a movie. When she helped us in the fields or came back from the fields.
When something good or bad happened. I called her 'My little rain forest.'

KIMIKO

This is embarrassing.

MIYAGAWA

This American is fun to be with.

KIMIKO

When you gang up on me.

DANIEL

How old was she when she first spoke?

MRS. MIYAGAWA

Very young.

MIYAGAWA

And very loud.

DANIEL

Toilet training?

KIMIKO

Please stop. In the fairytales, the prince kills the dragon, not the princess. Don't give him any more ammunition.

DANIEL

Now I see that it is true that if Kimiko were a playwright's wife, she would cry frequently.

MRS. MIYAGAWA

(*Laughing.*)
You really are a comedian.

MIYAGAWA

If you are trying to catch a glimpse of the little rain forest, she's grown a lot tougher now.

VELVA

Kim-chan, I hear you are making a bust of your father.

KIMIKO

It is just a small project, a way of spending time together.

DANIEL

How is it going?

KIMIKO

(*Waving her hand across her face in embarrassment.*)
I'm in the early stages. So far just sketches. I need to get the proportions right.

DANIEL

Colonel, I have some sketches she's done of me. She's good at caricature. She has drawn attention to my rudeness, clumsiness, and bad smell. Make sure you have the final say on the design before it goes to the foundry. I'd get a signed affidavit if I were you.

MIYAGAWA

A statue stands still and can't speak. I hope it will say nothing, and, in doing so, will speak well of me.
(*Moves his hands over his lips as if zipping them tight.*)

The doorbell rings. Kareshi enters.

KIMIKO

(*To the guests*)
You remember Kareshi, the former deputy police commissioner. He'll be joining us.

VELVA

Great. I feel so much safer knowing he isn't stalking us.

KIMIKO

He can be useful. He's an expert guide.

DANIEL

I bet he knows where all the bodies are buried.

NOMURA

Where do you recommend that we stop?

MRS. MIYAGAWA

Takayama is really a vacation place, a glorified playground for skiers, hikers, and people interested in the outdoors and traditional crafts. It's not what you would think of as a backdrop for a love suicide.

NOMURA

Yes. You wouldn't expect lovers to kill themselves at an amusement park. So we're looking for recognizable and somewhat eerie places that can serve as a backdrop for the story. Think gates of a temple or a bridge over rapids in fog.

KARESHI

(Excited.)

We could suspend Daniel over the rapids in a helicopter. I'd be willing to lower him in.

DANIEL

No thanks. I've seen what I came for—this old house with its statue.

KARESHI

Take a good look. This may be the only time you come for a visit. Living here would be impossible for you. There's no way you could make a living.

VELVA

(Coming to Daniel's aid,)

He has real talent in areas you'd never appreciate. A writer's first duty is not to make a living but to recreate a world that is more real than the one we know.

MIYAGAWA

Why reimagine the world or try to recreate it This world is a paradise if we only knew how to preserve it.

MRS. MIYAGAWA

Now there's a challenge. It's hard enough preserving ourselves.

DANIEL

(Suddenly taken by what he's hearing,)

Thank you all.

(He bows his head.)

Thank you. *Hontoni arigato gozaimasu.* [Really, thank you very much.] Now I can sleep well... It's not what I expected. But you are so much yourselves and have given me plenty to think about.

NOMURA

Have you thought of a fitting ending to the story.

DANIEL

I don't know how it will end. All I know is that it may not have anything to do with what I expect. I once imagined this place but now I have no illusions.

NOMURA

That's it. That's the heart of any story. The characters have their will, but the world exerts its own. So live as if you have nothing to lose but your illusions.... Do that and you'll keep us in our seats till the last frame. You may have a knack to write for the cinema after all.

NARRATOR

They continue to talk as if they have been friends for many years, as if Daniel's presence poses no threat. Soon it is time for the guests to leave, and they can only exchange the usual pleasantries as any guests who came and went, enlivening an afternoon.

VELVA

We'll have to go soon.

MIYAGAWA

Too bad you can't stay longer.

VELVA

Thank you so much for your hospitality.

MRS. MIYAGAWA

Don't mention it.

VELVA

I love your house.

MRS. MIYAGAWA

Enjoy the rest of your visit.

MIYAGAWA

Daniel, don't hesitate to stop by the next time you're in town. Bring the wife and kids.

DANIEL

I'll send you an aerogramme. We can be pen pals.

Scene 4: On location in Takayama

Kimiko is in the front seat of the Bentley beside Nomura, the driver. Kareshi sits behind him. Daniel and Velva are also in back, crushed against each other and Velva's extra luggage. In the background are projections of a highway cutting through mountains.

DANIEL

How much stuff did you bring? I thought this was an overnight.

VELVA

I have my makeup.

DANIEL

That's three pieces of luggage.

VELVA

The rest are clothes. I brought outfits for when we take photos.

DANIEL

What kind of outfits?

VELVA

The kind they wear in French movies to make quick changes.

Nomura turns on the car radio. We hear whimsical travel music such as the Lennon/McCartney song, "The Two of Us."

They arrive at the gate to the Takayama Hachimangu Shrine. The backdrop is a blow-up of a wide-angle photograph of the red gate of the shrine.

NOMURA

We can't park here.

KARESHI

Park as close as you want.

NOMURA

I don't want to get towed.

KARESHI

I'll take care of it.

> *Kareshi exits the car and pulls out of his pocket a yellow chalk line. With Daniel's help, he unwinds the chalk line and snaps it on the ground to form a yellow box.*

DANIEL

Now I see it.

KARESHI

The high stakes of police work?

DANIEL

No. Your most positive quality. You can improvise.

KARESHI

We might have been friends....

DANIEL

You mean, if we weren't rivals.

KARESHI

She's not choosing between us. It's whether she's going to get married at all.

DANIEL

You may have something there.

> *In front of the shrine's gate, Kareshi stands with Velva, Daniel with Kimiko, wearing sunglasses and sunhats. They blow kisses and wave to the audience as if they are movie stars. From a theatrical trunk they take out other hats, wigs, and festival costumes. Their movements are backed again by whimsical travel music.*
>
> *Kimiko and Velva wear festival clothes known as kamishimo. Kareshi wears a costume of the Shishimai dancers that makes him look like a fighting cock.*

VELVA
(*Grabs a new costume for Kimiko and Daniel.*)
This costume is for the Lion Dance.

NOMURA
Kim-chan, do you remember the steps?

KIMIKO
We perform it every year.

Kimiko and Daniel cover themselves under the multicolored lion costume.

KIMIKO
Follow my lead.

They bow, move their left leg, then their right, and bow, and repeat many times. Then they skip like children and do a tango. You can hear them laugh under the fabric.

NOMURA
This would make a great location. It's like a James Bond movie. You could hide in costume and escape, setting up a chase with a procession of floats.

DANIEL
(*Lifts his head out of the lion costume.*)
I'm not interested in the chase. I prefer the dance under the blankets.

Daniel grabs Kimiko to embrace her under the costume. They continue to dance to the travel music.

Taking off the costume, Kimiko and Daniel walk with the others to a dark part of the stage near the red gate where a food kiosk suddenly lights up.

MRS. ITO
Irashai. Irashai.

VELVA
(*Admires the selection of confections and drinks.*)
There is so much here.

MRS. ITO

What would you like?

VELVA

How about a pitcher of bean tea?

MRS. ITO

I also have sweet dumplings and cookies.

VELVA

No thanks. We're full.

DANIEL

Do you have Baked Takayama?

MRS. ITO

What's that?

DANIEL

It's like Baked Alaska. A cake covered in ice cream and meringue, doused with rum, and lit on fire. Only Baked Takayama burns to a crisp. A mountain of sweetness goes bitter and dark in a matter of moments.

KIMIKO

Stop it.

NOMURA

(*To Daniel.*)
You remind me of Lionel Barrymore in *You Can't Take It with You*. He blows up the house with fireworks. Would you take down an entire mountain to get your way?

DANIEL

If only it were that easy.

They walk back to the Bentley. Nomura drives to the next stop.

NOMURA

I'm exhausted.

KIMIKO

Daniel has that effect on people.

VELVA

It's been a whirlwind visit. I feel like a grandmother on the tour bus.

KIMIKO

Is bad grandpa behaving?

DANIEL

It's tight quarters. She's on my lap. My right leg is cramping.

KIMIKO

We'll stop again soon.

DANIEL

Velva, I've just noticed that your hair has tints of red. What color is it?

VELVA

Candy ginger with a touch of flame.

DANIEL

Talk about a firecracker!

VELVA

Where are we heading now?

NOMURA

Into the mountains.

KIMIKO

You'll be able to see my house from the trams.

Close with travel music.

Scene 5: The Ropeway

Their next location is the Shinhotaka Ropeway which runs across the Ontake Range in the Northern Alps. Kimiko and Daniel are thrilled that they have finally found a place to be alone. They are talking in the first car.

The gondola is an open car that could be made to look in flight by the demeanor of the passengers who hold onto the handrails while they peer into the distance.

Daniel and Kimiko can see the high crests of the Hida Range, and the river valleys dotted by small villages. The gondolas hang like charms on a bracelet across the valley.

KIMIKO
Finally we have some time alone and there are many things I want to say.
(Takes a deep breath.)
Watching you with Miss Ogata, I realized that I have never been strong enough to push back against you. I'm completely overwhelmed by you, by your emotions. You need someone like Miss Ogata, who is strong and protective. She would make a good wife for you.

DANIEL
We brought her here because we thought your father would be more comfortable with another woman as a buffer between us.

KIMIKO
I bet she's a good buff. She's lively and talented. She can't get enough of you.

DANIEL
I'm sure she wanted to test you—to see how you would react to someone who behaved more freely with me. Are you trying to say that you have completely given up on me?

KIMIKO
Do you know the fairy tale of the princess who must live forever in the Dragon Palace? She gives a boy she loves a keepsake box that he must never open, for when he does, he will find that 100 years have passed,

and he has become an old man…. What is left for us? You will peer into that magic box and find that the years have flown, and I am nothing more than a Dragon princess. I can't leave and you must go. I can do nothing for you. I should cut my hair like a nun who has renounced the world.

DANIEL

Give up on me but not on your future.

KIMIKO

(*Tears flow freely as Kimiko empties her heart to him.*)
I won't bear a child… for my father's sake. And I cannot bear…to satisfy… a husband's … constant desires… I can't please anyone.

DANIEL

(*Wipes her eyes with his handkerchief.*)
You've always pleased me, even now when you send me away. I'm sorry it's difficult for you.

KIMIKO

Ii-e. I am the one to apologize. *Gomen, nasai.* I'm the *doji*—the blundering fool—who can't do what anyone wants or meet their expectations. Call me Dojiko. That is the name I will take as a nun.

DANIEL

I'm sorry—I can't see you reading the sutras.

KIMIKO

You see me only through your own eyes. I don't want to marry. I will take care of my parents when they get old. I will run the farm by myself and do what I can with my art… You have a life. You should live it to the fullest. My life is constrained by my family. And by *my* choice.

DANIEL

For the longest time, the only life I could imagine was with you. I am a *doji*, too—a Tokubei—a puppet on a stage who comes to life only when I'm with you. There is no reason for you to apologize. We all blunder and stumble over ourselves. I'm glad we found each other for this long.

KIMIKO

You make it so hard for me...
(*She takes his hands and holds them to her.*)
These are real hands, not hands of wood. You once said that they were
your best feature.

DANIEL

They're made for scribbling and pulling myself out of awkward scrapes.

KIMIKO

I'm getting dizzy up here. I can see my village. It's so small and self-
contained. I'll grow old and ugly from farm work and the sun. I've already
begun to lose my luster.

> *Sound from offstage of a giant sputtering engine. Daniel and*
> *Kimiko look around from their seats to see what is happening and*
> *brace themselves.*

NARRATOR

The tram has stopped moving. Once more they are stuck in place, but this
time they have come to an agreement to move on with their lives. The
entire scene made the news that evening.

NEWSMAN

(*Narrator can be heard over speakers.*)
This is Radio One Nagoya reporting live from the Shinhotaka Ropeway. A
man is climbing the ropeway to save a young woman stuck in a tram car
800 feet above the ground. The rescue began when the engine sputtered
and the tram stopped moving.
(*Waving to Velva to come on stage.*)

With us is Nagoya's own Velva Ogata, the local actress who is often
typecast as the jilted lover or the innocent bystander. Velva, today you are
an eyewitness. Can you describe for us what is happening now?

VELVA

(*With a look of astonishment.*)
Detective Kareshi is climbing the cables of the ropeway a thousand feet
into the air across the valley to check on the safety of Miss Miyagawa... I
almost can't bear to look.
(*Peeking through her arms wrapped around her head.*)

NEWSMAN

He is closing in on the tram car where there is a woman and another man, He's barely a spec in the air moving across the cable. He is getting closer to the car suspended over the valley, moving handhold by handhold. Now he is reaching with a rope to tie himself to the car. What are you thinking as you see this, Velva?

VELVA

It's like watching the Great Wallenda…. Not even a stunt man would dare try it. There is no insurance company that would cover it.

NEWSMAN

He has reached the tram and is climbing into the box to rescue her. He's reached her and prepares ropes and clips to carry her away.

VELVA

We're watching a silent movie. We can't hear what they're saying to each other. But she doesn't want to go anywhere.
(*Excitedly.*)
She's a brave one herself. She'd rather stay in the tram than be carried off by a man.

NEWSMAN

It is as if the man has gotten the message. He's backing away now. He's climbing back down. He'd better hurry if the tram starts running again. He could be knocked into the valley.
(*Roar of the generator starting to sputter on.*)
He'd better get down fast. Look! He's made a zip line out of the cables!

VELVA

He's moving so fast.

NEWSMAN

And now the tram is moving again.

VELVA

I'm breathless just watching.

NEWSMAN

The cars are moving again. The rescue that wasn't a rescue has ended safely for everyone. This is Nagoya News One from the Shinhota Ropeway on Mount Ohtake. We'll be back after this commercial break. Stay tuned. Weather on the 8s.

Scene 6: Kareshi and the Colonel

It is sundown. While the visitors have gone with Kimiko to the inn for dinner, the detective reports to the Colonel in the Shoin room of the Miyagawa house where Kimiko had been working on her sculpture.

MIYAGAWA

Where is everyone?

KARESHI

They've gone to dinner at the onsen. If you can spare a moment, I'd like to report an incident.

MIYAGAWA

I heard there were two incidents. First the power went out. Then you played Tarzan. What were you thinking?

KARESHI

I was afraid the line would break.

MIYAGAWA

Kareshi, I know you're capable. I've seen the resume. Seven years in Search and Rescue. You could do something like that before breakfast. But all we needed was close surveillance.

KARESHI

Yes sir.

MIYAGAWA

I hear Kimiko refused your help.

KARESHI

I didn't know whether to take it as one more rejection, or whether she was just being protective of me.

MIYAGAWA

She cares for others more than for herself. Sometimes she freezes. When she was eight, she was afraid to come down from a persimmon tree after rescuing the cat.

KARESHI

Those two aren't particularly adventurous.

MIYAGAWA

Some thrills are overrated. I used to fly dawn raids to take out bridges and bunkers. Now I am beginning to appreciate a game of *mah jong*, which has no risk or strategy…. Anyway, our work will soon be over. The American is likely going back to New York, perhaps for the last time. One thing I've always wondered. Why don't American parents worry about their kids getting involved with someone from another country?

KARESHI

I hired a detective in the U.S. She said Daniel's family and friends were just happy that he found someone…. Anyone would do. Do you think something might happen tonight?

MIYAGAWA

They keep talking about love suicides. I'm afraid they may try to reenact a scene from one of Chikamatsu's plays. Are you familiar with them?

KARESHI

I slept through the classics in school.

MIYAGAWA

What did you take up in school?

KARESHI

Space. I was good at the things you don't test in school. Sports and keeping people out of trouble. I've done most of my learning on the job.

MIYAGAWA

(*Laughs.*)

Well, let me fill you in. In Chikamatsu's love suicide plays, the couples take a last stroll to commit seppuku side-by-side. It's usually not far from the father's house or the brothel where the girl lives.

KARESHI

I'll follow them in the fields and along the river. Do you want me to bring both back? I would be happy to dispose of Daniel.

MIYAGAWA

Just make sure there's no trouble.

Scene 7: At the bathhouse

The filmmakers are staying at a Takayma onsen, a bathhouse inn with an outdoor mineral spring that looks out over the Hida Range. Daniel is sitting in the bar of the onsen with Nomura as they wait for Kimiko's arrival.

DANIEL

I'm glad you're here. I wanted to show you. For a few years now, I've been learning to operate puppets for the theatre. Let me introduce you to Chikamatsu.

NOMURA

That's fine workmanship.

DANIEL

He's a gem. Made of hinoki cedar.

Lifts up the puppet so he stands on his feet. The puppet has a soft wooden face and wears a golden robe.

NOMURA

Does he speak?

DANIEL

He's a font of profane wisdom.

NOMURA

Then I will ask him profane questions.
(*To the puppet.*)
Chikamatsu-san. I bet you had a reputation with the ladies of the *makutsu*.

CHIKAMATSU

My nickname in the quarter was "Kuma"—the powerful but gentle bear who offered protection.

NOMURA

Did you have a special woman?

CHIKAMATSU

We called her '*Mochi-gome.*' Sticky rice. I couldn't get enough of her. She was the model for every woman in my plays. She loved fully and offered herself completely. I imagined hundreds of stories of men trying to bring her out in the daylight. By the third act, when they go outside to kill themselves, I could elevate the work to poetry.

DANIEL

You were a master of the last goodbye and the final stroke.

CHIKAMATSU

I allowed my characters to rejoice in that moment.

DANIEL

You were a sex fiend *and* a philosopher.

CHIKAMATSU

I'd probably be writing X-rated art films if I were alive now.

NOMURA

But everyone thinks you were so solemn.

CHIKAMATSU

In my work, I wore a dark coat, not this golden robe. I revelled in scenes where priests beat their acolytes and the commoners and samurai alike were knocked to their knees.

NOMURA

There were so many deaths. You burned through so much wood.

CHIKAMATSU

I couldn't save the lovers from themselves. Marriages were arranged, and men sought true love where they could find it—in the pleasure quarters.

Daniel continues to manipulate the puppet, making it rise and walk, and mug for the crowd. Kimiko enters carrying a note from the front desk, a long flower-patterned silk (katana) bag for a sword. Daniel flops Chikamatsu forward on his face and greets Kimiko with a big smile and a formal bow.

KIMIKO

Nomura-sensei. Your wife left a message at the front desk.

NOMURA

Thanks. I'd better check in.
>	(*Exits.*)

DANIEL

I was drinking with my friend here. Chikamatsu had a few too
many.
>	(*Makes a hand gesture of how the puppet fell flat on his face.*)

KIMIKO

What are you drinking?

DANIEL

Enough rum to do damage.

KIMIKO

What kind of damage?

DANIEL

I'm getting sentimental, which is poison for a writer. And now that I
am here at the bathhouse, I remember being a student in Kyoto. After
studying, I'd leave my boardinghouse to walk with you to the public bath
near Shijo-karasuma. You let me carry your purple bucket.

KIMIKO

You were still just a teenager. You dazzled me with your words. And
so serious—about me, about your plans.... Today, you made a lasting
impression. True to form, my father said, 'For someone who knows
nothing, you certainly are free with your opinions.' He called you a
tengu—a large, monstrous bird with a big nose who flaps around out of
control.
>	(*Peals of laughter.*)

Flap. Flap. Flap.

DANIEL

I have a nose.
>	(*Reaching out to touch her nose.*)

DANIEL (Cont.)

Yours is flat, like it was cut off by the retainer of Lord Musashi. Did your father like my friends?

KIMIKO

He said that they were loyal to you even when you flew off the handle.

DANIEL

I thought I was fairly restrained.

KIMIKO

Since when have you ever held back?

DANIEL

I didn't mention that my father, Al Singer, directed the angle, elevation, and trajectory of the anti-aircraft guns where your father's squadron flew. Dad's battery fired on your father's planes at Luzon.

KIMIKO

We might never have met.

DANIEL

We might never have been born.

KIMIKO

We might still be in the lotus fields. We would have been like Buddha, without a stain.

DANIEL

What did your mother think of me?

KIMIKO

She was charmed. She wasn't put off by your rough edges. She said you never give up, which means you will be successful at whatever you do.... She also said you are the type of man....
(Covers her face as she begins to laugh.)
who will get better looking as you age.

DANIEL

(Daniel winces.)
I've always had to work at self-improvement.

KIMIKO

Here's your reward for being a good soldier.
> (*Hands him the bag.*)

It's my father's sword. It proved useful alongside Oda, Hideyoshi, and Ieyasu, the unifiers of Japan.

DANIEL

I'm honored. I carried your bucket. Now I'll carry his sword.
> (*Takes sword out of its sheath to feel the blade.*)

The sword of the divider who separates us. The source of our dismemberment. It's not the ending I wanted. We will end this with poetry and a festival of blood.

Act III: The Michiyuki
(Final walk of the lovers)

The backdrop is the Miyagawa house at night below the bright moon and stars. At the right side of the stage there is the bright red Nakabashi Bridge and the sound of rushing water—the Miyagawa River. Daniel is dressed in an untucked, button-down shirt and dark cotton trousers. He carries Kimiko's father's sword in the traditional manner—the scabbard tucked into a sash at his waist. Kimiko is dressed in a green long-line silk tunic and jeans. In the background are the Takayama Mountains. They walk the perimeter of the stage as they talk and at the end of the scene enter the water together near the bridge together.

NARRATOR

They walk far from the house
along the Miyagawa River
to the vermillion-lacquered
Nakabashi Bridge that connects
the old city with the last vestiges
of feudal Japan.

They have lived like ghosts,
knowing they will soon be lost
to each other. Daniel knows
that there is no place for him here.
Life is a dream, an unconscious
world that doesn't last.

KIMIKO

Ah, did you hear the bell?
When it strikes nine it will be
my father calling me to bring his pills.
Tonight I am here with you
and will not serve him.

NARRATOR

As they walk in the evening mist, a light rain
falls that vanishes before it hits the ground.
They walk in the shadows of houses,
their steps and breathing as one.

DANIEL

Look, the moon is fast asleep,
hiding in its bed of clouds.
It is the same moon we knew long ago.
I still carry the moonlight in your bucket,
and have saved it for a night like this.

KIMIKO

It's so quiet. No one can hear us but the mute swans
in the whispering water.

DANIEL

The night will listen to our woes.

KIMIKO

You can trust the night to keep secrets....
I have had no life in years other than those
days we have shared. Our friendship
has lightened my darkest days and nights.
What will I do when you're gone?

DANIEL

You have been the drug that helps me sleep
and keeps me going. My greatest comfort
has been knowing that we share the same moon.

KIMIKO

I will learn from the moon how to stand
with her alone among the distant stars.

DANIEL

Tonight, she will lead us to our final landfall
on this journey to cosmic dust.

KIMIKO

I will leave this life of pain
no longer ruled by blind passion
and give up all worldly attractions.
I will flee the burning house
to find a new home in the Pure Land.

NARRATOR

They stand at the water's edge,
connected like the pine and holly
that grow together along the bank.
They can hear the water of the river surge
as they make their way to the Nakabashi Bridge
at Sanmachi Suji that leads to the old
courthouse of the Tokugawa Shogunate.

DANIEL

This is the place where sentences were given
and carried out with the firmness
of the executioner's sword. We must enter
the water here to meet the fate of the doomed.
This will be our last goodbye. Let our spent passion
speak. Let my desire for you be one last memory to savor.

NARRATOR

They kiss, and the tears they shed
fill each other's mouths like drops of water
from a sponge that moistens the lips of the dying.

KIMIKO

You have come into yourself.
You are no longer trying to win
every new challenge and are not shaken
when events don't break your way.

DANIEL

And you have set your own course.
Now it is time to join the river.

NARRATOR

He holds the sword and is ready
to do his part in one final,
symbolic act of love.

DANIEL

Let us haunt this place like warriors
killed in battle, whose lives passed
too quickly.
>   (*He removes the sword from his sash and then the scabbard.*)
It is time.

KIMIKO

You first.

DANIEL

No. You first.

KIMIKO

>   (*Laughing*)
Hai doozo. Please, I insist.
>   *She takes the sword and moves it along his chin and cheek.*

DANIEL

>   It's funny that we can laugh.

KIMIKO

Life is a comedy when seen from a distance.
With this blade I trim your beard,
so I can remember every contour of
the alien face I love.

DANIEL

Careful.

NARRATOR

The sword cuts his ear.
His blood spills into the water.

KIMIKO

My hands were shaking and I missed the spot.

DANIEL

My wound is salt for the river, dissolving like our love.

NARRATOR

Daniel leans above her and, with expert care,
cuts the first snippet of her hair
and places it in his sash for safekeeping.

DANIEL

This releases you from any obligation to me.
To give you up is sadder and lonelier than dying.

KIMIKO

I have made my duty my desire.

NARRATOR

Once more he takes the sword and cuts her lustrous hair,
the mark of her nobility.

A voice comes from offstage.

KARESHI

Stop. Stop where you are!

DANIEL

It is that dog, Kareshi. What is he doing here? No one comes between
lovers ready to renounce the world.

KARESHI

    (*Breathing heavily from running; repeatedly bows and apologizes
    to the audience*).
*Gomen-nassai. Onegai shimasu. Sumimasen. [Excuse me. Please forgive
me. I am sorry.]*

DANIEL

Don't you have a life?

KIMIKO

Can't we do anything without you sniffing around?

KARESHI

(*Speaks to Daniel*)
Put that down before you get hurt.

DANIEL

I am already wounded by the sight of you.

KARESHI

You must not harm her.

DANIEL

Why would I harm her or yield to you?

KARESHI

It would be my pleasure to hack you with that sword
till your blood flows like Hirayu Falls. But I must
protect you from yourself.

NARRATOR

They would fight each other to the death, but Daniel has already left this
world. His quiet renunciation gives him hope for the future.
(*In the background two men in black appear as silhouettes
against the backdrop.*)
They cannot help themselves. Their spirits—two swordsmen—fight
on land, on the bridge, and along the shore. At various points, each
swordsman knows advantage and disadvantage.

DANIEL

(*Watching the swordfight.*)
If we are fools for love, let us save our folly for love,
not for cutting throats. That is a fate for great
lovers, who will not be spared, not for rivals motivated
by the whims of one who rejects the world.
(*Daniel hands his sword to Kimiko. The silhouetted swordsmen
sheath their swords.*)
Leave us alone. After tonight, she is yours
as much as anyone's.

KIMIKO

I belong to no man.

DANIEL

I feel already as if I've had my hand
severed like Gonzo the Lancer.
Kimiko, I would ask you to tear
your blouse into bandages to bind
my wound, but I have asked
for too much already.

KARESHI

What pleasure can I take in this defeat?
After robbing the warren, the fox's only gloat
is the rabbit in his mouth.

> *(Kareshi walks off stage. You can hear him on the police band
> telling the police sergeant at the dispatch desk to bring backup
> and EMTs.)*

Sergeant. This is Kareshi. Send a squad car and an ambulance down to
the riverfront under the Nakabashi Bridge. There's an American of my
acquaintance who needs help. He is unarmed and may try to take his own
life. Put the psych unit on alert. I'm going to help him so he doesn't bleed
out.

POLICE DISPATCHER

(Initial feedback on radio followed by orders from HQ.)
Base to all units. We've got a wounded alien at Nakabashi. Possible suicide.
Send an ambulance and backup. Bring him in for observation.

NARRATOR

The river is flecked with blood from his ear as if with crimson leaves.

KIMIKO

O unlucky Tokubei. Your desires remain
unfulfilled. I hope when you return
to your homeland you will find someone
new to help you find what we could not
provide each other. Seek out a strength,
a power that can help you live. Now I am free
as a child is free, with no encumbrances.
I hope to come into your path in the next life
when we have cleansed ourselves of the sins
that have come before, whatever they were,

KIMIKO (Cont.)

that have made it impossible for us
to be together in this life.

My head is partly shorn, and I am at last
free to walk without being noticed as a woman,
and you are free of the burden of mismatched love.

DANIEL

(Holding his ear to stop the bleeding.)
And I deserve my name—Tokubei—
once more damned. For without you,
I am empty. I will no longer claim
your friendship. I will slowly forget you.
I must find another life to spur me on
till I can rediscover who I am....
I had hoped to make this end
a glorious moment where I could rise
above myself and see the night as the moon
sees the ocean or the red-tailed hawk
sees the field, undisturbed by the commotion
they cause. But my heart is a trembling wave.
I must leave this place for safer ground.

KARESHI

What are you doing—rehearsing your next play?
I can barely understand you. If you keep talking
I will kill you myself. I assure you, the dead
that I pull out of the water never speak.

DANIEL

I am dead already. I am nothing
now that Kimiko has taken her vows
as the priestess of the mountain.

KIMIKO

I will live but not live.
I have nothing to offer any man.
It is now my lot to care for my father
and mother in their old age,
to feed them from my hand

KIMIKO (Cont.)

when they cannot eat, with none
to care for me. I will manage the farm
when they are gone, harvesting
wild sesame seeds, my *shiso* tears.

NARRATOR

The breaking of so pure a bond is no triumph,
the pain of loss the more sad because
they were so well suited.

Guileless, Daniel climbed Hida's peaks
to bring the source of his heart's fire
down the mountain. Now he chokes

for having lost that smoky flame. He can only
capture her on the stage in scenes that repeat
his unfulfilled desire, knocking on a door

with no answer, brushing off the hurt
and stain, testing his ability to withstand
this polite and bruising land.

Perhaps Kimiko and Daniel
can still meet once a year
like the hunter boy and weaver girl

when the birds make a bridge
for them to cross
under the big-faced moon.

Their time together has run out.
He feels impotent, the boy with the box
aged a lifetime in this moment.

KARESHI

What is he talking about?

KIMIKO

I have words only for the silent swans.

DANIEL

Your silence will make you easy to recognize in the next life.
Your sacrifice will bring good luck for anyone who makes
your acquaintance. A sacrifice of life is a new beginning,
blessed by its loss. But I will not be one who seeks you
for my own purpose. You are no man's back to carry
his burden, nor nurse to care for him, nor object
to be desired, nor portion for his pleasure. Not even
a sacrifice to be saved. *Ja, neh.* Until next time.
　　　(Steps to the front of the stage.)
I have played this Daniel, this Tokubei,
and offered you the opportunity to share in
his shattered dream. His hopes for a life
with Kimiko have vanished. She will become
the past, a memory of long-ago, and he will
reinvent himself. What can we do when
the life we imagine crumbles but replay
the scenes in our minds, acting out what
did not go as planned. We must resign ourselves
from the perfect life that seemed our due
to enter the real life we stumble into.
It is our nature to fight and love and fall,
our fate to discover that the play may be all,
whatever meaning found in how we fail.

Jah, ne. Until next time, friends. Or until
I'm cast again as the lover who cannot gain
his prize, as if she was ever mine to win.

The stage is here to witness aspects of your own
lives in the stories we tell. To open our hearts
to our own unresolved struggles, and if nothing else,
to bring us in laughter and sorrow to the final song.

　　　(From the darkness there is a color in the sky of cherry, tangerine,
　　　and salmon as if the sunrise has already begun again, drawing
　　　attention from the moon.)

DANIEL

The moon casts her cold eye down.
Cold eye, what you gotta say?

DANIEL (Cont.)

She says to give your heart away;
you'll find another.

If you don't believe it, just pretend.
That sun will rise again.
Today was this world, a dawn
of pink and tangerine

with shades of suffering, starting over.
We'll make our final bow and see
each other, perhaps, in stories of your own,
played on the stage of what might have been.

<u>Owari / Fin / The End</u>

Acknowledgments

With special thanks to Jeffrey Ranbom, a former literary manager and managing director of several regional and New York theatres, for his guidance and support in the development of the play and for sharing, over many years, his knowledge of the theatre. He pressed me at every turn to get the dialogue right, to keep things tight, and encouraged me to exploit (within limits) the imaginary space of the stage. Any limitations that remain in this work are my own.

Special thanks to the theatre director and playwright Ari Roth for making valuable suggestions and encouraging me to publish this even before it has the benefit of extensive collaboration with a theatre company. And to Marek Pavlovski for suggesting numerous improvements and additional scenes before publication.

I am also grateful to a few people who were enthusiastic supporters of this work—the plein air painter Andrei Kushnir and Elizabeth Reid Wonka, who has long shared my interest in Japanese culture and literature.

Much gratitude also to Chikako Ikeguchi, who has taken time to translate the play into Japanese with her collaborators Aleksandr Sklyar and Taro Hudson. Thanks also to Angus Paul, who has had a hand as an editor of all my poetry books, and likewise to the poet and writer Larry Moffi, founder of Settlement House, who was my first publisher. And to Edward M. Thron, professor of English emeritus of the University of Wisconsin at Green Bay, who has always been available to share his perspectives and interests.

Thanks to Michael Molanphy who has designed the covers of my last three books and to Johanna Hjort for her photographs.

Thanks also to my editor, Christen Kincaid, and publisher, Leah Huete de Maines, at Finishing Line Press, who were willing publish a play at a publishing house focused almost exclusively on poetry.

Sheppard Ranbom is a poet and playwright and the author of three books from Finishing Line Press: *I Didn't Know Kyoto* (2023), a chapbook written in a Japanese style favoring immediacy, brevity, and unabashed feeling; the comic novella in verse, *Shadows of the Pines* (2024), which satirizes the poetry industry and presents the rich inner life of a poetry teacher who is aided by the spirits of poets of the past and tormented by his own words; and this play. He is also the author of the book-length poem, *King Philip's War* (Settlement House, 2008), which recounts the genocide of the New England Algonquians. His website can be found at *sheppardranbom.com*